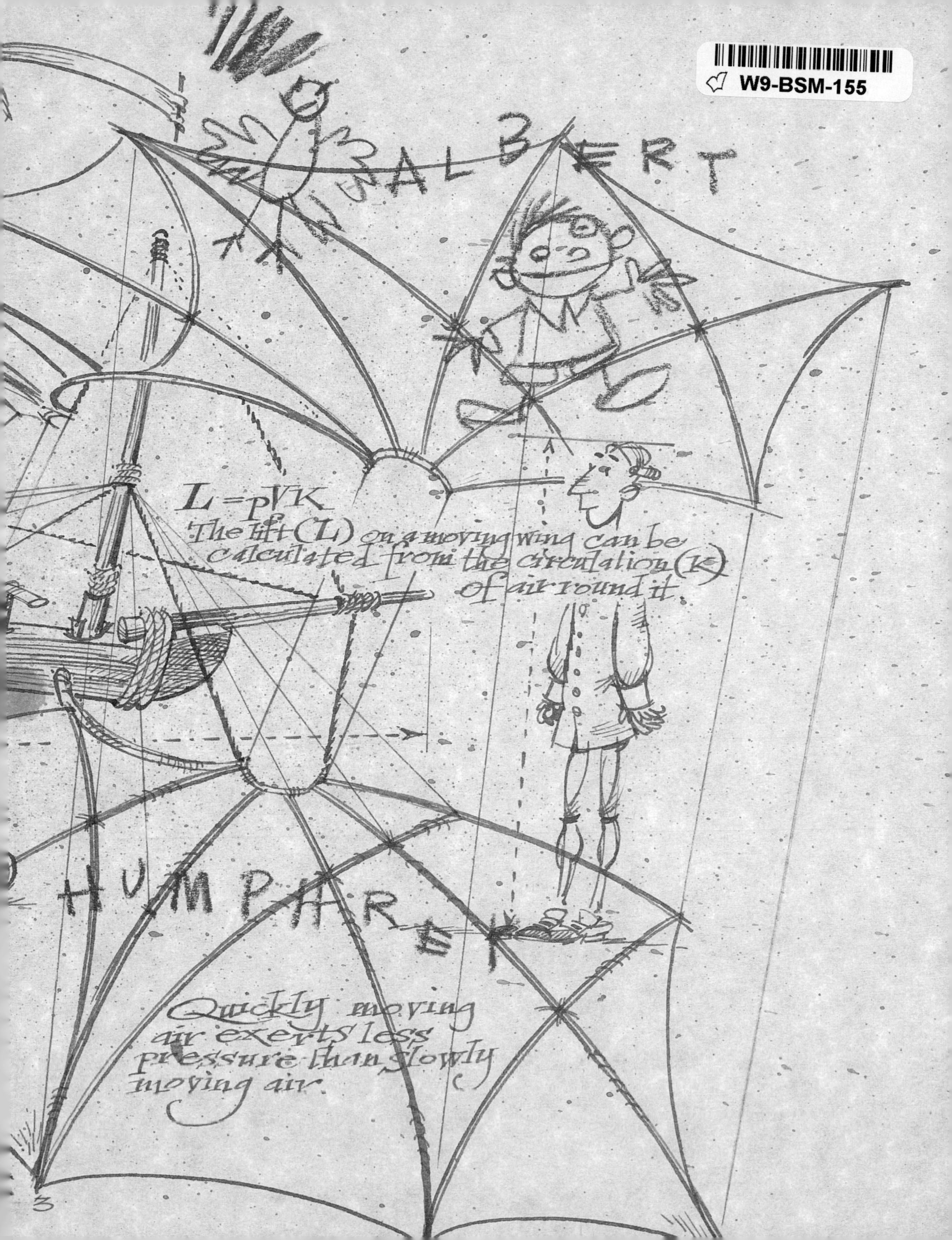
W9-BSM-155
ALBERT
L = ρVK
The lift (L) on a moving wing can be calculated from the circulation (K) of air round it.
HUMPHREY
Quickly moving air exerts less pressure than slowly moving air.
3

Humphrey, Albert, and the FLYING MACHINE

Kathryn Lasky

ILLUSTRATED BY John Manders

Harcourt, Inc.
Orlando Austin New York San Diego Toronto London
Manufactured in China

oday is Princess Briar Rose's fancy birthday party," Humphrey and Albert's mother said. "The event of the year! Of course, there's that silly rumor of the curse—the evil fairy and the hundred-year sleep and the kiss and all. But that's nonsense. No one would want to hurt sweet Briar Rose. Won't this party be grand!"

"No, it won't," said Humphrey. "It'll be the most boring party in the world."

"In the universe," added Albert.

"Clean up, boys," said their father. "We must look our best for court."

"I hate going to other people's birthday parties, especially princesses'," said Albert. "Boring!"

"There'll probably be dancing. I hate dancing," muttered Humphrey. "Boooring!"

"No more *B*-word, boys," their mother hissed.

The palace banquet hall was filled with sounds of celebration.

"Grown-up food," mumbled Humphrey as a servant set a gold plate in front of him.

"Probably fruitcake for dessert." Albert sighed. "Whoever heard of cake with fruit?"

"Look at Mother and Father dancing," said Humphrey. "How embarrassing."

Albert poked his brother. “Who’s that old lady trying to dance with the princess?”

“She’s kind of scary.” Humphrey pointed. “Look at that wart! And that hair in her ears!”

Just as the boys were thinking, *Maybe I'm not so bored now,* the princess tumbled into a heap on the dance floor. The king yawned. The queen yawned. The other dancers sank softly to the floor, snoring gently. Platters of food crashed as servants fell asleep on the spot.

Humphrey and Albert yawned enormous yawns. "Guess this is boring after all," they murmured, and fell fast asleep. The boys' prophecy had come true: This was indeed the world's most boring party. And so, too, the prophecy of the enchantment had come true: The princess had been cursed, and the entire court had fallen into a deep sleep.

An immense hedge of thorns began to grow. As the years passed, the entire palace became completely hidden by the thorns and brambly nettles. In time the legend of the enchantment spread far and wide, and no one really knew anymore whether the curse was true.

Ninety-nine years, eleven months, and three weeks later, Humphrey and Albert woke up.

"Look at all these cobwebs!" Albert exclaimed. "How long have we been asleep?"

"About one hundred years if the prophecy of the curse is right," Humphrey said. "That must be what happened. But I think we woke up a little early."

"You mean that boring story Mother told us? About the princess?" Albert whispered in amazement. "I thought she was kidding!" He did some quick math. "That means you're one hundred and ten years old. And I'm one hundred and eight!"

They looked around the ballroom. Everyone was still sleeping deeply.

"Looks like it's our job to wake everyone up," said Humphrey.

Humphrey and Albert tried to wake their parents with gentle nudges and pokes. They slept on. Albert shook the king's shoulder. Nothing. Humphrey sprinkled pepper under the queen's nose, but she just sniffed in her sleep. Albert threw a bucket of water over the prime minister's head, but he only burbled and snored.

"Wait!" Humphrey lifted a finger. "Doesn't the story say that everyone will wake up only if someone kisses the princess?"

"Yech!" Albert made a face. "Don't look at me. You do it."

"Not us! A handsome prince. Or if we can't find a prince, maybe just someone handsome. Let's go."

Before the search could begin, the boys had to cut their way through the thicket of thorns. They took swords from the sleeping knights and began hacking and whacking.

"This is better than dancing," said Humphrey.

"Definitely not boring," Albert agreed.

Getting through the hedge took hours, but finally the boys set off down the road to find a handsome man. Before long they'd spread the word throughout the nearest village, posted a sign, and waited for the crowds to arrive.

Young men, old men, and middle-aged men began to line up. Humphrey and Albert interviewed each one. Some were bossy, some meek. Some were chatty, some silent. Some were fat, some skinny. Some were even handsome. But they were all very boring. The brothers decided that the last thing a court that had been sleeping for one hundred years needed was a bore, even a handsome one. Everyone might fall right back to sleep.

"Maybe we should try the next village," Humphrey said. "People there might be less boring."

"Yeah, who cares about handsome," said Albert.

"Looks aren't everything," Humphrey agreed.

So they headed down the road.

As they walked past a field, the boys spied a mysterious sight. They raced over for a closer look.

"*Magnifico! Wunderbar!*" A man was almost singing as he danced around a strange contraption.

"What are you saying?" the boys shouted. "And what is that thing?"

The man clapped his hands. "*This* is my flying machine!"

"Flying machine!?" Humphrey and Albert exclaimed.

"Yes, yes! Are you not excited, boys? We are on the brink of conquering gravity. I wish to enter the realm of enchantment!"

"The what?"

"The palace, dear boys. I want to fly over that hedge of thorns and see the cursed palace. People say that the entire court has been sleeping for one hundred years. If I can make it over the enchanted hedge, my flight will be the ultimate triumph of science over charms."

Humphrey and Albert looked at each other.

"He's not too fat," Albert whispered. "And not too thin."

"He's not handsome," Humphrey said, "but he's definitely not boring."

"Could we fly with you?" Albert asked the man.

"Can you pedal?" he said. "I mean *really* pedal. Getting this thing to fly takes energy—and a lot of it. And you can't stop pedaling. If you get tired, if you get bored, if you stop pedaling, we crash."

"That's exciting!" the boys cried. "*Magnifico! Wunde*—what?"

"*Wunderbar!* Wonderful, wonderful!" the man shouted. "Ah, what quick learners you boys are. First you'll have to help me make some changes in the wings because when we calculate the pounds per square inch of lift in relation to the speed of the airflow over the upper curved surface of the wing—"

"You mean we have to make the wings bigger," Humphrey interrupted.

"Or else we won't lift off," Albert added.

"Exactly!" And the fellow bounced a bit on his toes. "Oh, by the way, my name is Daniel Bernoulli, and I'm glad to have you both aboard! Let's get to work!"

So the boys helped Daniel enlarge the wings of his flying machine. They worked for two days building thin branches into a frame, stitching silk, and weaving harnesses.

But their first test flight was a failure. After a few seconds in the air, they plunked down with a thud.

"It's not working!" Albert wailed.

"What happened?" cried Humphrey.

"No whining, please," Daniel scolded. "We are inventors, scientists. Only evil fairies whine. Back to work!"

The boys worked alongside Daniel for the next few days. They did not whine. They did not complain. And they were *never* bored.

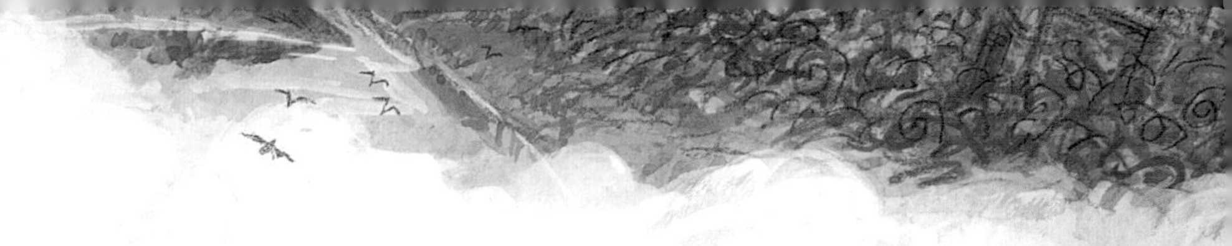

Finally they were ready to try again. They went to the crest of the hill. Set to fly, they waited for a strong gust of wind.

"Get ready, kids!" Daniel shouted as the wind blew hard. They felt themselves lifting off, and the flying machine began to rise. The boys pedaled with all their might.

"We're flying!" cried Albert as they saw haystacks turn to the size of anthills and trees become green specks below.

"Magnifico!" they all shouted.

Soon both boys were sweating and their legs were aching. They were so tired, they thought they might fall out of the flying machine before they ever made it to the palace.

"Onward, boys! Keep going. You are magnificent! We are nearly there!" Daniel called over the wind. And Humphrey's and Albert's legs found new strength.

They skimmed over the enormous wall of thorns. As they approached the palace, Daniel shouted, "Okay, boys, let go the spoilers!" Humphrey and Albert untied two kites that unfurled behind them. As they landed gently in the courtyard, a terrible silence surrounded them.

"This way," Humphrey said. They went past a sleeping guard and entered the great hall. Briar Rose lay where she had fallen one hundred years earlier, with partygoers sleeping all around her.

"What do we do now?" Albert whispered. "Should we tell him the kissing part?" For once Humphrey had no answer.

But Daniel wasn't paying attention to the boys. He had spotted the princess, and his eyes glistened.

"Oh no!" Albert muttered. "He's crying. He'll never kiss her."

Daniel clasped his hands to his heart and sighed. Tears rolled down his face.

"He's having a heart attack!" groaned Humphrey.

But Daniel's tears were tears of joy. Never had he seen such beauty. He ran toward the sleeping princess and kissed her ever so gently.

Briar Rose's eyes opened. And for the first time in a century, a butterfly in the palace courtyard began to flutter its wings. The king rolled over and the queen stirred. Then the entire palace started to rustle. A jester yawned and turned a somersault, and Briar Rose and Daniel gazed into each other's eyes.

Briar Rose had never in her life seen anyone with such a noble face. "Are you a prince?" she asked.

"No," he sighed, "only an inventor."

"An inventor? How exciting!" Briar Rose imagined elaborate designs and calculations spinning through Daniel's mind. In that mind she saw beauty, and in his eyes she saw love. "You are the handsomest man I have ever met!" she gasped.

In a dark corner of the great hall, a woman with a huge wart on her nose hopped on one foot, then the other. "Handsome?! His ears are lopsided. His nose is crooked. And he's not even a prince!"

"He *is* a prince!" Humphrey cried.

"A prince of science!" exclaimed Albert.

The curse was broken forever! The evil fairy dissolved into a muddy little puddle and drained away. And Daniel Bernoulli reached for the hand of his beloved Briar Rose.

Not too many days later, Humphrey and Albert's mother shouted, "Boys! We can't be late for Princess Briar Rose's wedding to Master Bernoulli. Won't it be grand!"

Humphrey and Albert looked at each other.

"Grand? Who cares about grand?" said Humphrey. "We know it won't be boring!"

"Not with Master Bernoulli!" said Albert.

So the princess and the inventor were married and lived in happiness for the rest of their long lives. Humphrey and Albert grew up to be fine inventors themselves—and they were never bored again.

A NOTE FROM THE AUTHOR

Although this story is a fairy tale, drawn from *Sleeping Beauty* and my imagination, one character is based on a real person. Daniel Bernoulli was born in 1700 in Groningen, the Netherlands. During his lifetime Bernoulli lived in many places, including Switzerland, Italy, and Russia. Although his parents wanted him to be a merchant, Daniel wasn't interested. His father was a mathematician, and it was math that Daniel really loved. At age thirteen Daniel entered Basel University in Switzerland, where his father taught, and studied philosophy, logic, and higher mathematics. He later studied medicine.

Daniel was especially interested in the physics and mechanics of movement—the movement of all things, from water in a canal to blood and air in the human body. One of the most important results of his exploration of movement was the discovery of a principle that later led to the invention of the airplane. Daniel realized that the faster air flows over a surface, the lower the pressure is on the surface. If an airplane wing is constructed so the air flows faster over the top than the bottom, then the pressure on top of the wing will be less than the pressure below the wing, and the wing will be forced upward. This principle, now known as the Bernoulli Effect, makes it possible for something heavier than air to fly. In my story I imagine that Daniel's discovery leads to his invention of a flying machine. However, the real Daniel Bernoulli died in Switzerland in 1782, more than one hundred years before the first airplane left the ground.

For Matthew, again—K. L.

For Uncle Dennis and Aunt Dorris—J. M.

www.HarcourtBooks.com

Library of Congress Cataloging-in-Publication Data
Lasky, Kathryn.
Humphrey, Albert, and the flying machine/Kathryn Lasky; illustrated by John Manders.
p. cm.
Summary: In this takeoff on the Sleeping Beauty story, two bored boys awake before others in an enchanted castle and set off to find a handsome prince, only to end up with an ingenious inventor named Daniel Bernoulli.
Includes a note on the real Bernoulli.
[1. Fairy tales. 2. Princesses—Fiction. 3. Inventors—Fiction.] I. Manders, John, ill. II. Title.
PZ8.L3287Hu 2004
[E]—dc22 2003018151
ISBN 0-15-216235-6

First edition
A C E G H F D B

The illustrations in this book were done in watercolor, gouache, and pencil on watercolor paper.
The display lettering was created by John Manders.
The text type was set in Stone Serif.
Color separations by Colourscan Co. Pte. Ltd., Singapore
Manufactured by South China Printing Company, Ltd., China
This book was printed on totally chlorine-free Stora Enso Matte paper.
Production supervision by Sandra Grebenar and Pascha Gerlinger
Designed by Judythe Sieck

THE FLYING MACHINE.

DANIELIS BERNOULLI, JON. FIL.

A B C E F

Air flowing over the top of a curved wing must travel farther, & so must travel faster.

Propulsion

X.

Z.

Y.

Lift.

figure 1.

Fast-moving flow

Slow-moving undisturb'd flow

This pattern of air flow may be illustrated by streamlines; velocity (V) and pressure (p) changes are given here:

$$p + \frac{1}{2}\rho V^2 = \text{constant}$$

dynamic pressure